TULSA CITY-COUNTY LIB

S0-BOB-574

baer

Dear Parents:

Congratulations! Your child is taking the first steps on an exciting journey. The destination? Independent reading!

STEP INTO READING® will help your child get there. The program offers five steps to reading success. Each step includes fun stories and colorful art or photographs. In addition to original fiction and books with favorite characters, there are Step into Reading Non-Fiction Readers, Phonics Readers and Boxed Sets, Sticker Readers, and Comic Readers—a complete literacy program with something to interest every child.

Learning to Read, Step by Step!

Ready to Read   Preschool–Kindergarten
• big type and easy words • rhyme and rhythm • picture clues
For children who know the alphabet and are eager to begin reading.

Reading with Help   Preschool–Grade 1
• basic vocabulary • short sentences • simple stories
For children who recognize familiar words and sound out new words with help.

Reading on Your Own   Grades 1–3
• engaging characters • easy-to-follow plots • popular topics
For children who are ready to read on their own.

Reading Paragraphs   Grades 2–3
• challenging vocabulary • short paragraphs • exciting stories
For newly independent readers who read simple sentences with confidence.

Ready for Chapters   Grades 2–4
• chapters • longer paragraphs • full-color art
For children who want to take the plunge into chapter books but still like colorful pictures.

STEP INTO READING® is designed to give every child a successful reading experience. The grade levels are only guides; children will progress through the steps at their own speed, developing confidence in their reading.

Remember, a lifetime love of reading starts with a single step!

TM & © 2021 Nintendo. All rights reserved. Published in the United States by Random House Children's Books, a division of Penguin Random House LLC, 1745 Broadway, New York, NY 10019, and in Canada by Penguin Random House Canada Limited, Toronto.

Step into Reading, Random House, and the Random House colophon are registered trademarks of Penguin Random House LLC.

Visit us on the Web!
StepIntoReading.com
rhcbooks.com

Educators and librarians, for a variety of teaching tools, visit us at RHTeachersLibrarians.com
ISBN 978-0-593-30444-0 (trade) — ISBN 978-0-593-30445-7 (lib. bdg.)

Printed in the United States of America
10 9 8 7 6 5 4 3 2 1

Random House Children's Books supports the First Amendment and celebrates the right to read.

MEET MARIO!

by Malcolm Shealy

Random House New York

MARIO

Here We Go!

Mario is a cheerful person
who is no stranger to adventure
in the Mushroom Kingdom.
The Mushroom Kingdom
is a peaceful place.
But when there's trouble,
Mario can be counted on
to save the day!

LUIGI

Okey Dokey!

Luigi is Mario's
friendly brother.
Luigi tries to be brave,
but he is timid—
and afraid of ghosts!
Even so, he is willing
to join his brother on
any adventure.

DONKEY KONG

Going Bananas!

Donkey Kong is known
for his great strength
and red tie.
Bananas are Donkey Kong's
favorite food.

YOSHI

Big Appetite! *GULP!*

Yoshi is laid-back
and likes to eat fruit.
He helps Mario
by using his long tongue
to gobble up enemies.
He can flutter his legs
to jump really high
and avoid danger.

Toad Time!

Toad is one of the citizens
of the Mushroom Kingdom.
He is loyal, cheerful,
and polite.
He's always happy to help
Princess Peach
whenever he's needed.

PRINCESS PEACH

Perfectly Peachy

Peach is the princess of
the Mushroom Kingdom.
She tries many things,
including adventuring, sports,
and kart racing.

Princess Power

Daisy is the princess
of Sarasaland.
She is full of energy.
She also enjoys playing sports
and kart racing.

ROSALINA

Mysterious Friend

The mysterious Rosalina
came from outer space with
little Luma, the lost star child.
With her powerful star wand,
Rosalina is always calm
in the face of danger.

TOADETTE

Happy and Hardworking

Toadette lives in the
Mushroom Kingdom.
She is brave and always
ready for adventure.

21

BOWSER

KING KOOPA

Mario's biggest and baddest foe
is Bowser.
With his pointy horns,
his fiery red hair,
and the spiky shell on his back,
Bowser is also the mighty
King Koopa!

BOWSER Jr.

Like Father, Like Son

Bowser Jr. is Bowser's energetic son.
He wears a bandanna painted
to look like a monstrous mouth.
He thinks it makes him look older!
Bowser Jr. is mischievous
and more than a little naughty.

KOOPALINGS

The Koopa Crew

Armed with magic wands and other powerful weapons, the Koopalings are trusted and devoted helpers of Bowser.

Wendy

Lemmy

Morton

Iggy

Roy

Ludwig

Larry

Their names are Lemmy, Wendy,
Morton, Iggy, Roy, Ludwig, and Larry.
Wherever there's a disturbance,
the Koopalings are
almost always involved!

MINIONS

Mighty Minions!

Only Bowser's mighty minions stand between him and Mario. Bowser's minions can be found everywhere—marching in fields, hiding in pipes, and even swimming underwater!

Koopa Troopa

Spiny

Kamek

Piranha Plant

Lakitu

Goomba

Bowser may be a lot of trouble,

but Mario's friends

gain courage

and stand up to Bowser

when they hear

Mario say . . .